My Best

Friend's Brother

Part 2

Victoria Hall

Dedication

Heavenly Father thank you once again for blessing me with book #3, Father there was no way I could have done this without you. I thank you for giving me the opportunity to proceed with my first dream. I want to thank, once again my sister in Christ, LaKeya Guy for being patient with me and encouraging me. I want to thank her team for publishing my books. I want to thank my children Frankie, John, Tangela, and Tracey for all of their support and for encouraging me to continue on writing books. I want to thank everyone for all of your support in buying each book.

TABLE OF CONTENTS

CHAPTER ONE

I t's been 3 months now since Lisa laid Jimmy to rest. "Hello, hey Lisa how are you?," asked Bianca. "I'm good, still in shock of what's going on here, I spoke with the Detectives that are on the case and they have no lead", cried Lisa. "Bianca, I miss him so much, I need Jimmy here by my side," says Lisa, with bitterness in her voice. "Why did they take away my first love from my daughters and me?"

"Lisa, why don't you and the girls come and spend next weekend here with the kids and I, we will be happy to have you here. You have been in that house for three months feeling sorry for yourself," says Bianca. "Lisa, you know that Jimmy's murder wasn't your fault right?" "Yes, Bianca, I know but I'm the one that told him to stop driving around with his gun in the car, just in case he gets pulled over, I'm the one that took it out of his car while he was in the house getting dressed," she cried.

"Lisa, you weren't wrong for what you did. With Jimmy out there riding dirty and carrying a weapon, yes, if he was to get pulled over, they were going to lock him up. So yes, Lisa, you did the right thing," says Bianca.

Lisa's other line buzzed, "Bianca let me call you back. I have another call." Okay girl make sure you call me back.

Hello, hey Lisa, it was Mimi on the other end of the phone, "hey Mimi what's up?" I was calling to see how you were doing, and how the girls were doing. "Mimi, it's hard for me right now," cries Lisa, "every time I look at Jymayia I see Jimmy, Mimi she looks as if he carried her himself". Lisa and Mimi talked for about an hour, after the conversation was over both ladies said their goodbyes and hung up.

Lisa picks Jymayia up and hugs her crying, Jymayia I'm going to find out who took the love of our life away from us, I promise you that. Lisa and her daughter lays down to take a nap before she has to pick Narlyn up from the caseworker's office. After Jimmy was killed Lisa decided that she would let Nook take Narlyn one weekend out of the month to spend time with her. She felt that was her daughter too and as a mother she would never take the child away from their mother.

It was 5 pm and Lisa pulled up to the office of the caseworker. She sees the caseworker and Nook standing outside talking. Lisa gets out of the car and walks over holding Jymayia in her arms. Nook's face turned a shade darker once she saw Lisa walk over to her, Nook has never seen Jymayia until today. Narlyn is Jimmy's daughter as well but she looks just like Nook, and Nook hated that her daughter doesn't look anything like Jimmy. Lisa puts a smirk on her face as she walks up, Narlyn runs over to Lisa, and wraps her arms around Lisa's legs. If looks could kill Nook would have killed everyone that was standing out there including her own daughter.

"COME OVER HERE NARLYN!"

Nook yelled, the caseworker looked at Nook, but didn't say anything, but Lisa did. "Nook please don't yell at her like that, she's just happy to see me that's all", Lisa said with a smirk on her face. Nook looked at Lisa and said, "this is my child, not yours and I will say what I want to say to her, you worry about that thing you got in your arms" she said. Lisa just smiled at Nook, Lisa asked the caseworker if the visit was over and can she take her girls home now. "Your girls?!" Says Nook, "listen little girl Narlyn is not your daughter and if you keep acting the way you're acting you're going to be laying next to your dead baby's father". The caseworker looked at Nook, she seen the anger in Nook's eyes.

As Lisa was walking to her car she turned around with this I'm a kill this girl look on her face but the caseworker made Nook get in the car. Lisa put the girls in their car seats, tears are coming down Lisa's eyes as she gets into the car to pull off.

They pull up at Terri's house but Lisa just sat there in the car crying. Terri comes out the house and sees Lisa in the car, she walks up to the car and sees Lisa crying.

"Lisa what's the matter she asked?" Lisa snapped out of her thought and asked Terri can she help her get the girls out of the car. After they took the girls out of the car Lisa told Terri what Nook said to her. "Wait, Lisa, what did she say?" Terri, I don't want to jump to any conclusions but if this girl had something to do with Jimmy getting killed or if she did it herself Terri she has to go and I mean that.

A car rides down the street with tinted windows, the car slows down, the window comes down slowly, it was Nook, Myia and Tiffany laughing. Lisa got up to run to the car and Terri grabbed her. Nook laughed and pulled off. Lisa crying screaming at Terri, "WHY DID YOU GRAB ME TERRI?" Lisa sat down on the steps rocking back and forth. Terri had never seen her best friend like this before, Terri takes the girls that are now crying in the house to her mother.

Terri comes back out, Lisa you have to pull yourself together for the girls, they shouldn't have to see you like this. Terri hugs her best friend and tells her that their family is going to find out who did this to Jimmy. "Kyle, and Raheem are on it they not going to let whoever did this live trust me Lisa," says Terri.

At this point, Lisa didn't want to hear anything Terri was saying to her, she wanted to fight Nook and her friends. "Terri, I need to get away for a couple of days," Bianca said, the girls and I can come and stay at her house next weekend. Terri didn't say anything, she took it that her brother didn't tell Lisa everything about his life and now wasn't the time for Terri to tell her either.

Terri wanted to tell Lisa everything since Jimmy wasn't here, but she just hugged her best friend tight while Lisa cried in her arms. Terri, I miss him so much, if it wasn't for me taking his gun out of the car he would still be here, Terri I didn't want him to get pulled over and the cops find his gun on him. Terri, it's all my fault why Jimmy is going. Lisa, it's not your fault and you have to stop blaming yourself for Jimmy's death. I have to go, Terri, I need to go home and lay down. "Will you be alright driving back to Philly like this Terri asked?" "Yes, I will be alright, can you get the girls I don't want your mom to see me like this" says, Lisa.

Terri brings the girls outside and helps Lisa put them in their car seats, she hugs Lisa and watches her pull off. "Lisa, why are you crying?" Narlyn asked, "Sweetie, I'm okay I just got something in my eyes," replies Lisa as she wipes her face.

Lisa and the girls get home and as she takes the girls out of the car her phone ring, "Hello" says Lisa, click, the person hangs up. The phone rings again but this time Lisa didn't answer it. After she gets the girls fed, bathed them, and lays them down for bed. The phone ring again, this time Lisa picks up the phone and starts yelling "STOP CALLING MY PHONE!!, if you got something to say, then say it".

"Excuse me" says Bianca, Lisa got quiet, who is this she asked. "It's me Bianca," she replies, "oh hey girl what's up, is you okay" asked Bianca? "Yes, I'm okay" says Lisa with an attitude. "Someone keeps calling my phone and hanging up and it's bothering me, Bianca. First, this girl says that I'm going to be laying next to my dead baby's father then she rides pass me with her friends laughing like your daughter didn't lose her father as well". "Lisa, listen don't pay her no mind maybe that's just her way of dealing with the fact that her daughter's father is going."

"Bianca let me call you back this is the detective on the other line," says Lisa. "Okay," says Bianca, "make sure you call me back girl". Lisa lied to Bianca, there wasn't another call on the other line, Lisa just wanted to sit and think about all that has happened in the past 2 weeks. Lisa lays in her bed thinking about what is going on, she falls to sleep. See Lisa wasn't no dummy, her father taught her a lot about the streets at a very young age, and Jimmy also made her aware of different things because of what his life style was.

"Ring Ring Hello" says Lisa, you thought this was going to be over with says the caller on the other end of the phone and then hangs up. No one has my number but my family, Terri, Bianca and Jimmy's family she thought to herself. Lisa mind is racing all over the place right now. Lisa's phone starts ringing, she just looks at it saying to herself I'm not in the mode for the games today.

"Hello" she answered. "Hey Lisa this is Kyle, I'm calling to see if you need anything," "you know what Kyle I do need something" says Lisa. "Okay little cousin what is it?" he says, "how well do you know Bianca she asked?" Kyle didn't answer right away, "hello," "yeah I'm here". "She's my man's girlfriend," says Kyle, "what's up why you asking about her?." "Nothing, I just have a lot of thoughts going through my mind right now" says Lisa. "Okay but what does Bianca have to do with this if you don't mind me asking,' says Kyle. "It's nothing Kyle I just want to know who killed Jimmy that's all". "Wait and you think she did it or had something to do with it."

"Lisa that's Jimmy's right hand man and his best friend's wife. I really don't think she would do anything like that to Jimmy, she treated Jimmy like that was her brother too. Yeah, I'm over here tripping Kyle you right" says

Lisa. "Yes, get all of them bad thoughts out of your head and let us handle this, okay?" says Kyle. "Okay, I got you," says Lisa as she tells him bye.

Lisa picks the news article up and starts to read it, "I don't care what Raheem, Kyle or Terri says I'm a find out who did this to you Jimmy," as she starts reading the article before falling to sleep. It's now 9 am and the girls are woke, Lisa cooks breakfast for them, gets them dress and heads out to Norristown, Lisa didn't tell anyone she was coming because she needed to take care of some business, Lisa drives pass Dekalb Street just to look around and see if there was anything that the cops had missed.

Lisa pulls over, before getting out of the car she says to Narlyn, "stay here in the car, I will be right here in front of the car," she says. Lisa gets out of the car, as she is walking around looking on the ground for some type of clue, she spots an earring, she picks it up and puts it in her pocket and gets back into the car and pulls off. I know I seen this earring before she thought to herself but just couldn't think of who she seen wearing it. She calls Terri and tells her that she was in Norristown at her mother's house and that she was coming over so the girls can see their grandmother.

Lisa pulls up to Terri's house, the next door neighbor and Terri were sitting outside. Lisa gets the girls out of the car, Narlyn runs over to her aunt and gives her a hug. "Hey girl," says Lisa, as she sits in the chair next to Terri. "Hey is you okay?," Terri asked. "Yes, I'm okay just got a lot on my mind right now," responded Lisa as she puts her head down in the palm of her hands. Lisa didn't want to tell Terri that she was looking for answers to what happened to Jimmy, Lisa also wasn't going to tell Terri that she found an earring where they found Jimmy's car the night he was killed. She didn't want anyone to think that she was tripping over the lost of Jimmy. Lisa didn't know what to think or who to trust at this point. Lisa needed answers right now and she was going to do everything in her power to get those answers.

Terri was talking to Lisa but Lisa wasn't listening, she just sat there looking at her daughter with a tear in her eye. "Lisa, you can't keep worrying yourself about this, you're going to get yourself sick."

Lisa snapped, "TERRI YOU ACT LIKE YOU DIDN'T JUST LOSE A BROTHER THE SAME WAY I LOST A FATHER TO MY DAUGHTER!!" she said yelling. Lisa and Terri had words back and fourth with each other, "Lisa, yes that was my brother and yes I'm hurt just as well as you're hurt Lisa, because he's not here anymore but I know my cousins will take care of this. You really need to pull youself together Lisa, you're taking your anger out on everyone and we don't deserve it Lisa."

Lisa says crying, "Terri that was the only man I ever been with that I fell in love with and now he's not here for his daughters or me Terri so if I'm angry I have all the reason to be angry." Terri puts her arm around Lisa, Lisa it's going to be alright please understand that Kyle and Raheem got this.

CHAPTER TWO

The weekend is here, Lisa gets her and the girls ready to go and spend time with Bianca. She pulls up to the house as she was about to knock on the door, the door opened and it was Tina walking out, she stopped and looked Lisa up and down, then put this smirk on her face and walked to her car. Before she got in the car she turned back to look at Lisa and started laughing.

Bianca comes to the door, she looked like she was crying. "Hey Lisa, come on in," says Bianca as she wiped the tears from her eyes. "What's going on?" Lisa asked as she walked into the house. "It's nothing Raheem is cheating on me again with his other baby mom and we just got into it, he packed some of his clothes and left right before you got here." "Will you be alright?" asked Lisa. "Yes, I will be alright this isn't the first time we got into it and he left."

"Lisa, sometimes I wish Raheem was more like Jimmy was, he loved you, he did everything and anything in the world for you." "Bianca, I am sorry that you're going through this with Raheem and I really don't know what to say about this because I never experienced what you're going through." "It's okay Lisa, he will be back once he cools off." "Where's the kids at?," Lisa asked. "They are in their room." Bianca takes Narlyn up to play with her daughters, Jymayia was sleep so she stayed downstairs with Lisa.

Bianca sits on the sofa next to Lisa, "girl I didn't think you were coming she said with a little grin on her face?." "Bianca, I had to clear my head a little, I told you what happened when I want to pick Narlyn up." "Yes, you was telling me, so what did you say when she said that to you?," Bianca asked with this weird look on her face. "Bianca I really wanted to run over to her and smash her head into the car window, but I had the girls and plus after she said that to me, the caseworker rushed and told Nook to get in the car."

"After all that, I told you how Nook and her girls came down the street laughing like I'm sweet," says Lisa.

The door opened and then closed, Raheem walks in the living room. "Hey Lisa," he said as he sat down beside her to give her a hug. Bianca didn't like the fact that Raheem was sitting there with his arms around Lisa like that. "Raheem, can you please let us talk?," says Bianca as she gives him this look, Raheem took his thumb and wiped a tear away that was in Lisa's eye.

"Why did you come back Raheem?," says Bianca. Raheem just looked at her and grabbed his keys and walked out the door.

Bianca sat down on the sofa where Lisa was but on the other end, Lisa's head was down, Bianca just sat there and stared at her with a look on her face. Lisa lifted her head, "Bianca can I ask you a question?" "Sure what's up?," "If Jimmy only slept with your girl two times then why is she acting like they were in a relationship with each other?. Why was she acting the way she was with me? And she doesn't even know me. And she bite Jimmy in his neck then going to press charges on him because he smacked her?"

Bianca almost choked trying to clear her throat to answer Lisa's questions. "Lisa, to be honest with you I really don't know how many times Jimmy and Tina slept with each other," says Bianca, knowing that she was lying to her. "Was you out there when Jimmy and Kyle want to the car?," she asked. "No, Raheem and I were still in the backyard. We heard yelling so we came out to the front and Tina had her hand in Jimmy's face, Jimmy was trying to common her down by pulling her close to him," lied Bianca.

Lisa turned to look at Bianca with a look on her face, she knew that Bianca was lying cause Jimmy always told her that he would never lie to her and she believed it, but Lisa didn't say nothing. Lisa put her head down like as if what Bianca told her was hurting her. "Bianca, why would he lie to me?" says Lisa, "Jimmy told me that he would never lie to me and I believed him." "Bianca, I believed everything that he told me." Bianca just sat there looking at Lisa.

"Knock Knock" It was the front door, Bianca got up to answer the door and it was Tina at the door laughing. "Is Jimmy baby mom still here?" she asked laughing. "Bianca, I hate that girl, and Jimmy got what he deserved," says Tina as she picked up her sunglasses that she left on the kitchen counter.

Bianca already told Tina that Lisa was coming to spend the weekend with her, but she also told Tina that the kids were going to be coming to so don't try anything. "B, listen Jimmy should have watched what he did to me, hurting my feelings as if it was okay, and 'B' it's not okay," Tina said as she started crying. "This man really thought he can dog me out like that and get away with it, no 'B' he can't," she said talking loud. "Tina you need to leave," said Bianca, "I don't want nothing to happen between you and Lisa here in my house, not why the kids are upstairs." "Okay 'B' I will leave but you just let her know that her man will never hurt me ever again," says Tina as she walked out of the house slamming the door shut.

Tina gets into her car a speeds off down the driveway. Bianca walks back into the living room and sees that Lisa is giving her a look. "Who was that asked Lisa?"

"Oh that was Tina she forgot her sunglasses and she was telling me about her and her dude was fighting." Lisa knew that Bianca was lying because she heard the whole conversation, Lisa played it off and just laughed to herself. 'That girl just can't win with men, can she?," says Lisa. "I guess she can't," says Bianca under her breath as she walked back into the kitchen.

"Lisa would you like something to drink?," asked Bianca. "No, I'm good," says Lisa thinking to herself "this girl really think that after what I heard that I am going to trust her to give me something to drink?. I'm glad I feed my kids before we got here." Now Lisa has all kinds of thoughts running through her mind, she didn't know what to think.

Jymayia woke up and she started to cry, Lisa picked her up out of her stroller. Jymayia was very pretty, she had long curly hair, her eyes were the same color as Jimmy's eyes were. Same nose and lips, when Lisa took her out of the stroller Bianca almost dropped her glass. When Lisa came in the house Jymayia was turn on her stomach so Bianca really couldn't see her face.

Lisa sat down on the sofa and asked Bianca, can she breast feed her daughter. Bianca cleared her throat before she answered, "sure" she said, looking at Jymayia saying to herself this baby looks just like Jimmy and she is so pretty she thought to herself.

Lisa can see that Bianca just kept staring at her daughter, so she started laughing a little, "what's the matter Bianca?" Lisa asked. "Lisa your daughter is so pretty and she looks as if Jimmy spit her out, she looks just like him. His other daughter doesn't look nothing like him," says Bianca. "Did he take a blood test with his other daughter?" Bianca said, if you don't mind me asking. "Yes, he took a test with her, he actually took two tests, one he took on his own and then the courts made him take a test also."

After Lisa was finish feeding Jymayia she asked Bianca if she wanted to hold her, Bianca didn't know what to say she just sat there in a daze looking at her like she had seen a ghost or something. "Bianca, you good?," asked Lisa. "Yes girl, I'm good it's just she looks like I'm looking right at Jimmy and it had me stuck for a minute." "Yes girl, I be feeling the same way when I look into her eyes, its like Jimmy is sitting there watching me, and Bianca, all I can do is cry because she will be laying on the bed beside me just looking at me and smiling like she is doing now." Jymayia just kept looking at Lisa smiling at her with this beautiful smile on her face.

"Bianca, she's such a good baby too, the only time she cries is when she is wet or hungry and she sleeps all night. You miss your dad, don't you?," says Lisa as she played with Jymayia's little fingers. "Oh wait Lisa the phone is ringing," says Bianca, she gets up to answer the house phone and it was Raheem's baby mother on the other end, the two ladies get into a heated argument where Bianca ends up slamming the phone down. Lisa gets up and walks into the kitchen and she sees Bianca standing there crying. "Hey girl, is everything okay," Lisa asked. "No, it's not okay, Raheems baby mother just called and we got into an argument. Lisa I know he is still messing with this girl just by the things that she was saying on the phone Lisa. I love Raheem and will do anything in the world for him, I just wish he was more like Jimmy was with you," says Bianca.

Lisa just stood there looking at Bianca wondering why she keep saying that she wishes that Raheem was more like Jimmy. Bianca walks into the living room telling Lisa how she caught an STD from Raheem and how he made a baby on her and that was the reason why her and the baby mother keeps going at each other because she knows that he is still dealing with her. "Bianca, how do you know that he is dealing with her, he can be telling you the truth about him not messing with her." "Lisa, the baby is 3 months, he still goes and sees this baby, and how I know that he is still messing with her or someone else because he barely sleeps in the bed with me. He comes home yes he does every night but must nights he goes into his office and will be in there all night."

"Bianca, that does not mean that he is cheating." "Lisa, you're young and you have a lot to learn about these men." "Bianca all I know is that Jimmy was good to me and if and when the time comes that I will see another man I will make sure he is just like Jimmy or better. Men will be men

Bianca and I'm just glad that I had a good man and now someone took him away from me and I really don't know why," says Lisa turning the focus back on her so she can see how Bianca reaction will be.

Lisa really doesn't know who killed Jimmy, in her mind she thinks it was Nook because of how Nook is acting. Lisa gets calls every now and then telling her that she was going to be next and that she will be laying beside her dead husband, all Lisa can remember is when Nook said that to her when she had picked Narlyn up last week. Lisa really doesn't think that Jimmy had any enemies but Nook and Tina. Lisa doesn't know if he had any enemies in Philadelphia that would have followed him up here and killed him. But why would they come all the way up here and kill him Lisa thought to herself.

"Lisa, Jimmy did his dirt trust me, and if you really think that him and my best friend had two nights together you're sadly mistaken. I know every time Jimmy would come out here and Tina was here they would talk to each other," lied Bianca. "He will never treated me bad," says Lisa. "Yes, you right he didn't treat you bad and that's why it hurts Tina cause he made it seem like they were a couple to her. Listen Lisa, I know you don't believe me because Tina is my friend and that Jimmy told you he never will lie to you but there was more to him and Tina's relationship then he was telling you, and I am not only saying it because she is my girl either."

Lisa turned to look at her girlfriend Bianca in the eyes and said, "then tell me why you felt the need to say all that you have just said, Bianca". See Bianca really don't know Lisa as well as Raheem does, Raheem seen Lisa in action the night of her birthday party.

"Lisa I'm just saying, my girl is hurt because of how Jimmy treated her, and yes she said that she was going to have her brother come to Philly and see him." Lisa looked at Bianca and said, "so Tina had her brother come and kill my daughter's father, is that what you is telling me Bianca." "No, that's not what I am telling you, Lisa. To be honest I really don't think that she told her brother cause of the fact that she fell in love with Jimmy."

Lisa's mind is racing all over the place right now, Lisa knew in her heart that Jimmy wouldn't lie to her and that she believed everything that he has told her. But Lisa played it kool she wanted to beat the breaks off of Bianca and leave her there for her kids to find her but Lisa took the conversation in a different direction.

"Listen Bianca, I'm not going to say that you're telling the truth about all of this and Jimmy isn't here to say it's the truth or not so I'm a leave that alone. I just want them to find who his killer is before I do," says Lisa as she walked out of the living room and up the steps to go and get her daughters. "Lisa, you don't have to leave, it's late and I don't want you to drive home with the girls this time of the night."

"Bianca, right now I really don't trust being around anyone at this point. Bianca I will be alright, I thought that I can come here and get away from all that is going on around me. Then I come here and you tell me that my husband was messing around with your friend and that it was more than two times like I am supposed to believe that?." Lisa takes the girls to the car and straps them in the car before going back to the front door to tell Bianca something. "Bianca, I really don't care who Jimmy was messing with, and if I find out that Tina or her brother had something to with the death of my daughters' father you can say goodbye to your friend and her brother," says Lisa as she walks back to her car and pulls off.

When Lisa pulled up to the house she sees Raheem standing outside of his car. At first Lisa just sat there thinking why was he at her house when he knew that she was at his house. Lisa gets out of the car but leaves the girls in the car while she walked over to Raheem to see why he was at her house. "Hey Lisa," says Raheem. "Why is you standing here at my house Raheem and you knew I was in Jersey at your house?, asked Lisa.

"Your neighbor called my phone and told me that it was someone at the door, no one knows where Jimmy lived so I came here to check it out." "Okay then, why he didn't just call me?," says Lisa with a look on here face still wondering why Raheem was here. He said, "he called you and your phone want to voicemail, besides he was a little drunk too when I pulled up," says Raheem not looking at Lisa while he was talking.

Lisa looked at her phone, "Raheem I don't have any messages on my phone at all, if he called me he would have left a message and I don't remember turning my phone off while I was at your house Raheem." "Listen, Lisa I just came here because he called my phone, so I came to check it out and that was it, I didn't go inside or anything. Matter fact I just pulled up right before you pulled up. Lisa you have to stop tripping," says Raheem. "Kyle and myself will make sure you and the girls are good, we still don't know who did this to my brother, Lisa."

Lisa looks at Raheem, "yeah, you right I am tripping she says, I got a lot of things racing through my head Raheem I feel like I can't trust anyone." "Lisa, you can trust me, that was my brother, my right hand man and I will kill for him so I'm the last person that will try to do something to him." Raheem puts his arms out to give Lisa a hug, but when Lisa gave Raheem a hug she felt that the hug was strange. She felt he was too close on her hugging her so she let go real fast.

"What's the matter?," asked Raheem." "Nothing" says Lisa as she walks to her car to get her daughters out of the car. "Do you need a hand?," asked Raheem. "No, I'm good, I can take them in the house myself." "Okay Lisa I will keep checking up on you to make sure that you and the girls are good," says Raheem. "Thank you," says Lisa as she takes the girls in the house locking the door behind her. Lisa puts the girls to bed, she sits down in the living room thinking, it's 11:00 o'clock at night, "why was Raheem here this late?," Lisa asked herself.

Next morning Lisa calls her father and talks to him about all that happened in the last two weeks. "Lisa, do you think that Raheem would do anything to his right hand man? Loyalty means a lot when your in the drug game, Lisa." "Dad, I know but it was kinda strange that Raheem was here at the house so late last night," says Lisa. "Raheem told me that the neighbor called him and told him that someone was at the front door. I asked him why would the neighbor call him and not me?, says Lisa to her father. I was up in Jersey at his house with his wife Bianca and get this dad she was telling me that Jimmy was more into her girlfriend Tina then, what he has told me."

Lisa's father asked, "do you believe her?" "No dad I don't believe her, and when I took Jymayia out of the stroller the look on Bianca's face was like she seen a ghost dad, it was scary the way she was looking at my daughter." "Lisa you might be thinking too much into this, that it has you going crazy, Lisa I don't know those people like that but if Raheem was loyal to Jimmy the way you say he was, then why would he kill him,' asked Lisa's father.

"Yes, you right dad I'm over here tripping." Lisa didn't tell her father about the earring that she found or she didn't tell him about what Nook said to her. After her and her father talked for a little bit Lisa told her father that she loved him before she said goodbye.

CHAPTER THREE

Lisa headed to Norristown to drop the girls off to Ms. Kaye, Jimmy's mother. After that Lisa went to the Courthouse in Norristown to get her gun licenses, then Lisa went and brought her a gun. Lisa didn't tell her father or anyone else that she had brought her a gun. Lisa felt that everyone thought that she was tripping and that Jimmy's death was taking a toll on her and that it had her thinking crazy thoughts. But Lisa knew within these two weeks that she wasn't tripping. Now it was time to put a plan together to find out who killed my husband Lisa thought to herself.

As Lisa was pulling up to Jimmy's mother's house she sees Terri outside arguing with someone, Lisa pulls up and jumps out of the car and seen that it was Nook that she was arguing with. The next door neighbor was trying to hold Terri back, Lisa ran over to swing at Nook but before she can get a hit in she felt this sting on her back, Lisa turned around and saw Tiffany with a stun gun in her hand pointing it at Lisa. Lisa ran toward Tiffany and grabbed her around her waist so she didn't have the chance to use the stun gun again. Lisa threw her to the ground and started punching Tiffany until she started bleeding. Terri pulled Lisa off of her, Lisa was crying and all you seen was fire in her eyes. Lisa snatched away from Terri and ran over toward

Nook but before she can get to her the police pulled up. Terri grabbed Lisa and pushed her in the house.

Ms Kaye came running down the steps asking what is going on, she sees Lisa crying and punching the wall. Ms. Kaye want outside, she asked the officers "what was going on?." Terri told her mother that, "Nook and her girlfriend came around here wanting to fight her and that they tried to jump her. And Lisa came, and Nook's girlfriend Tiffany stung Lisa with a stun gun. Lisa snapped and started punching Tiffany in her face, I told the officer that Lisa was defending herself.   The officer put Tiffany in handcuffs, they took her down to the police station." As Nook was about to get in her car she said to Ms. Kaye that, "Lisa was mad that her husband and your son was dead as she pulled off in her car laughing."

Terri said "when I see you Nook it's on," Terri went in the house, Lisa was sitting on the couch hands bloody and tears coming down her eyes. Terri put her arm around her best friend, Lisa cries in Terri's arms. 'Terri I know Nook killed my husband, your brother Terri." "I know she did," screams Lisa. Narlyn comes down the steps and runs over to Lisa and stands in between Lisa's legs and puts her arms around her and starts crying. Lisa pulls herself together once she realized that Narlyn was in between her legs. She hugs Narlyn tight, she tells her that everything will be alright.

Tears comes to Terri's eyes, Lisa asked Narlyn to go back upstairs with her sister so her and her aunt Tee Tee can talk. "Lisa, you have to pull yourself together for the girls, Narlyn is at the age that she will ask questions Lisa so you have to be strong for the girls."

Ms Kaye comes in the house and sees that Lisa is crying, She sits down beside Lisa and tells her that everything will be alright. "Lisa you can't drive yourself crazy over this." Lisa looks at Ms Kaye and her best friend Terri and snaps, "YOU'LL ACT LIKE HE WASN'T YOUR SON AND BROTHER!! I LOST MY FIRST LOVE AND THE FATHER OF MY CHILDREN," screams Lisa.

"Ms Kaye, I miss my husband," she said crying, "and I know Nook had something to do with his murder Ms Kaye, I know she did, why does she keep harassing me and telling me that I am going to be next?," cries Lisa. Terri looks up and sees Narlyn sitting on the steps crying, she walks up the steps and takes Narlyn back into her mom's room and tells her to stay in the room Lisa will be up there to come get her in a minute.

So as they finally common Lisa down, Ms Kaye want upstairs with her grandchildren. Lisa asked, "Terri can she take her for a ride to get the girls something to eat." As they was walking to Terri's car Lisa sees this Black truck with dark tinted windows slowly drive down Green Street and makes a right turn to go up Marshall street, she tried to look in the truck but the windows were to dark. She didn't say anything to Terri, she just got in the car. "So where did you want me to take you?," asked Terri, as she started up her car. "Take me to Lou's so I can get Narlyn a Cheese Burger," says Lisa with a low voice.

Lisa slides down in her seat a little puts on her shades and looks out the mirror that is on her side. She puts her pocketbook on her lap, Now Terri is looking at Lisa thinking, she really is tripping right now. As they go to pull off Lisa sees the black truck turn from Chestnut Street on to Green Street, she puts her hand in her pocketbook. As they turned to go down Marshall Street to Arch, the truck also turned, but it was driving real slow.

"Terri, turn on Arch Street then go up Moore Street," says Lisa real common, "Lisa is you alright?, asked Terri. Lisa didn't say nothing, as they made the turn onto Arch and then onto Moore Street the truck also made the turn as well. They got to the corner of Walnut and Moore about to make the right turn but Lisa stopped Terri. "No, make a left and then another left onto Marshall Street and pull over at that corner store please, I have to get something," she says.

Now Terri is getting worried about her best friend, but she did everything that Lisa asked her to do. As they pulled up to the corner store Lisa gets out of the car real slow but her hand was still in her pocketbook. Now the truck is at the stop sign on Marshall and Arch Street. Lisa goes and leans up against the wall and puts her phone up to her ear like she was calling someone. The truck slowly drives past her, Lisa looks again to see if she can see who was in the car. Lisa gets back in the car and asked Terri to take her to Conicelli. Terri looks at her like "what, hold up Lisa what is going on?, she asked her. "Terri please just drop me off there and I will call you after I'm done to come and pick me up." Terri didn't ask no questions but thought to herself what is going on and why Lisa didn't want to go right to Lou's.

So Terri took her to the Car Dealer and dropped her off, "Terri please go straight home and call me once you get in the house." "Okay," says Terri feeling scared for her friend now. "Terri make sure you check all your mirrors and make sure no one is following you, okay?." Now Terri is from the hood, she's from North Philly, But Lisa was also from the hood but seen a lot more than Terri seen. Terri's mother moved Lisa and Jimmy to Norristown when they was young. But Jimmy taught Lisa a lot before he got killed.

Terri was confused as to what was going on with Lisa, when she got home she called Lisa, "Hey, is you good," asked Terri. "Yes, I'm good just need to switch my car out." "You want to tell me what is going on?, asked Terri. Lisa got quite for a second, "Terri I will explain everything to you a little later, right now I can't because everyone thinks I'm going crazy," says Lisa in again a low voice. "Lisa we are here to help you, you can talk to me or my mom about whatever is going on." "Terri I can't right now, I will explain everything to you when it is the right time, Okay?," says Lisa.

Lisa gets a call, "Terri I will call you back when I am ready for you to pick me up," says Lisa as she hangs the phone up. "Why does she want me to pick her up if she is switching her car?" Terri thought to herself, "and if her car is here! What is going on with Lisa?" Terri asked herself.

Lisa answers her phone and it was Bianca on the other end, "hey, girl what's up?," say Bianca. Lisa was quite, "Hey, Bianca what's up?," she finally said. "Lisa is everything alright?," laughs Bianca. "Yes everything is alright I will call you back in an hour, okay?, says Lisa as she hangs the phone up. Bianca looks at her phone and says, "no she didn't just hangup on me." She calls Lisa back and the phone want to voicemail, she called her again and this time she left a message telling Lisa that they need to talk for Lisa to make sure that she calls her back.

Lisa never told Bianca that the night she left her house with the kids that Raheem was at her front door, and that he gave her a hug in an appropriate way. And that he has been calling her asking if she needs him to come over, if she needs someone to talk too. She wanted to tell Raheem about the earring that she found up there on Dekalb Street, she thinks hard, "I know I saw that earring somewhere but I don't remember where and who had it on."

"Lisa," says the salesman, he had to call Lisa twice, she snapped out of her thoughts. "I'm sorry sir, I was thinking about my husband, I apologize" says Lisa, "okay we have paperwork for you to sign and once we get all of that is done you can drive away in your new car."

The salesman gave Lisa the keys and she drive off, Lisa called Terri and told her to bring the kids to the Movie Theater on the Ridge, "Terri if you see a car or truck following you just go to Lou's get the food and call me when you get there" says Lisa. "Lisa, what is going on? asked Terri. "Not right now Terri, trust me I will tell you everything later but not right now." "Okay Lisa, we're leaving now, okay hang up call me when you get closer to Lou's." "I just want to make sure no one is following you." "Lisa is someone going to hurt me or the girls?" asked Terri. "No Terri I think you will be good," "then why am I looking for someone following me" asked Terri?

Lisa sighed real loud, "Terri listen please just make sure no one is following you please and call me once you get closer to Lou's."   Terri gets in the car and pulls off, she looks out her rear view mirror as she is driving, she doesn't see a following her. She calls Lisa and tell her that everything was clear. "Okay, I will see you when you get here Terri" says Lisa, "but please keep watching."

Lisa phone rings with an unknown number, Lisa doesn't answer it she sent the call to her voicemail. The unknown caller called again and this time Lisa answered the phone but didn't nothing. "Hello," says the caller, it was a males voice on the other end. "Hello" replied Lisa, "who is this?, she asked. "Hey Lisa it's Brick," Lisa pulsed for a second, "Brick how did you get my number?' she asked with an attitude, "and why is you calling me with an unknown number?." "Oh my bad that's just the way that I have my phone setup, I'm sorry I should have took that off my phone before I called you." Once again Lisa didn't say nothing. "You there?," Brick asked, "yeah I'm here" she replied back.

"How did you get my number Brick?, she asked again. "Jimmy used my phone to call you one day, he said that you was going to call back but you didn't so I just saved the number in my phone" says Brick. "Is that ok?, I know my brother would want us to check in on you." "Brick I'm good, the girls are good, I'm just a little tired and I want to get some sleep," she said. You home yet? he asked. Lisa looked at the phone thinking how he know I'm not at home. "No, I'm not at home," she replied. "Okay, just call me if you need anything, money whatever I'm just a phone call away," he said. "Okay, I will," Lisa said and hung the phone up cause she sees Terri pulling into the parking lot.

"Now you want to tell me what is going on Lisa?", says Terri. "Terri once I figure everything out I will tell you what is going on" says Lisa. Terri replied, "Lisa I am your best friend if something is going on I want to help you." "I know and I thank you for that, but this is something that I have to figure out by myself Terri. And once I get everything that I need I will fill you in," says Lisa as she was putting the girls into the car.

"So what is you going to do about your car that is at the house?," asked Terri. Lisa looked at Terri with a look, "Terri listen please let me just do this, there is a lot going on right now and I have to figure all of this out and I have to do it by myself. I really don't need you to keep asking a lot of questions, I know you want to help but Terri I can't involve you in this right now," Lisa explains.

Terri gets into her car a speeds off, Lisa get into her car and sits there thinking, Jimmy would never call me from his boys phone, and how did Brick know that I wasn't at home, I wonder if that was him following me in that black truck Lisa thought to herself.

Lisa calls Terri as she was driving, "hello," answered Terri. "Hey girl, I am so sorry that I snapped on you earlier, but Terri you have to trust me with this, once I figure all of it out I will let you know what is going on. I don't want to say to much cause I don't want you to say anything to Kyle or Raheem. Terri it's a long story but I'm trying to put pieces together of who killed Jimmy and at this point I really can't trust anyone. I know your my best friend and that I can trust you but I need you to let me handle this for right now. I know things are sounding and looking weird right now but I just need you to be here for me when I need you to be and not ask to many questions."

"Okay Lisa, please just watch your back and be safe, I'm here if you need me," replied Terri. As the ladies hung up Lisa's phone rings and it was

Bianca, Lisa didn't answer the call right away, she waited to call Bianca back once she got on the highway to go to her dads house. Hello, answered Bianca, "Hey it's me what's up?" 'What did we have to talk about?" says Lisa. "Lisa, I was just talking with Tina and she thinks that she is pregnant by Jimmy," Lisa was quite on the phone. "Hello," says Bianca. "Yeah, I'm still here," replied Lisa. "Yeah she called me crying saying that she had sex with Jimmy the night before he got killed, she said that she meant him in Norristown like he asked her too and they ended up sleeping with each other." Lisa still wasn't saying nothing, "Lisa, I am sorry to have to tell you this news," says Bianca. "So was she in the car with Jimmy when he was killed?," asked Lisa. "No, she wasn't in the car, they was at a hotel, he told her that he had to make a run and she said he never came back. I guess once Jimmy's mom found out he was killed they called Kyle and then Kyle called Raheem and that's how I found out he was dead. I called Tina and told her and she started crying."

"So if all this is true Bianca why she said that she was glad that he was dead and that he had to learn the hard way," Lisa said with angry in her voice. "And why is you even calling me with this Bianca I really don't care that she is pregnant Bianca, Jimmy is not here anymore so there is no need for you to call me about this girl anymore. If she is having his baby tell her to figure it out how she is going to take care of it," says Lisa and she hangs the phone. Lisa's mind is all over the place right now, she doesn't know what to believe, in her heart she knows that Jimmy wasn't cheating on her, but the conversation her and Bianca just had played in her head until she got to her dads house.

When she pulled up to the house her dad was sitting out on the porch, he got up to help her with the girls in the house. After Lisa had put them to bed she came downstairs to where her dad was at, She sat down and broke down crying to her dad, she had already told her dad some of the story as to what was going on, and now she told her father that the truck was following her and Terri. She also told he dad that Bianca said that Jimmy has a baby on the way.

CHAPTER FOUR

A week had gone by, Lisa and the girls were still at her dad's house, Lisa had cut her phone off for a whole week, Lisa thought to herself that she needs some rest from all that was going on right now. When she had turned her phone on, she had 27 missed calls and over 50 text messages. She called Terri back as soon as she heard her messages.

"Hello" answered Terri. "Hey Terri," says Lisa, "Lisa where are you?," "I've been calling your phone and leaving messages for you to call me back. Girl it's been a week where have you been." Lisa looks at the phone and thinks to herself, this girl really asks a lot of questions. Lisa had to laugh to herself before she responded to Terri, "Terri I'm good I had to get away for a little, I felt like I was going crazy being around the people who Jimmy had dealings with, so I had to leave and get away to clear my head," says Lisa.

"Terri did you know anything about Jimmy and this girl Tina asked Lisa?" "Lisa to be honest with you I never met her, Jimmy never took me anywhere near Jersey or New York, and if we ever went to New York it was to go shopping. I've never been to any of Raheem houses" replied Terri. "So you never met Raheem's wife Bianca then?" asked Lisa, still fishing for answers. Terri really wanted to tell her best friend the truth but she didn't have the guts to right now. "Yes, I know Bianca" says Terri. "So how do you know her if you never been to their house?" asked Lisa. "Lisa, Bianca is from Norristown," replied Terri. Lisa got real quite, "she's from Norristown?" asked Lisa. "Yes, she lived down her all her life until she met Raheem, Lisa, Bianca is our age," says Terri. Now Lisa is really confused to what to believe right now.

"Terri on my way home from the car dealer Bianca called me and told me that this girl Tina was having Jimmy's baby," says Lisa. "Lisa, I really don't think that my brother had any dealings with Tina like that, when he met you he stop going around a lot of his friends so I really don't think that he was at Raheems house like that. Besides Lisa, Jimmy really loved you, I don't think he would have slept with her again knowing what type of person she is. You have been with Jimmy long enough to know that he doesn't do drama or drama females. Lisa that's one of the reasons why he fell in love with you because you wasn't drama. I don't know what Bianca is trying to start but if that girl is pregnant trust me it's not Jimmy's," says Terri.

Lisa thinks to herself that Terri has a convincing story, and that she is going to go with it right now, but she thinks Terri is not telling her the whole story. "Terri the girls and I is on the road right coming to Norristown, I need you to pick us up in my car, I will tell you where to meet me at once we get close," says Lisa. "Okay," Terri was about to ask another question from Lisa but she thought I better not. "Terri pick them up at Plymouth Meeting Mall, and Terri please make sure no one is following you," says Lisa as she hangs the phone up.

Terri pulls up to the Mall but she doesn't know what entrance to go into so she just pulls into a parking spot and waits for Lisa to call her. Lisa is sitting in the cut in another parking lot watching Terri, she's making sure no one followed her to the Mall. Lisa walks up to the car and opens the back door to put the girls in the car, as she opened the door she scared Terri a little. "Oh, hey" says Terri as she watches Lisa strap Jymayia in her car seat. Lisa said nothing, "I know you hate when I ask questions but Lisa I want to know what is going on with you. Why is you being so rude towards me like I did something wrong to you?" says Terri.

"Lisa you have been snapping on me a lot and I just want to know why that's all, I know you're going through a lot and no matter what as your best friend I'm still going to be here for you, but I can't have you talking to me any kind a way Lisa, says Terri. "Terri, I'm sorry that I am taking my anger out on you." says Lisa as tears rolls down her eyes, "I'm trying to keep myself together that's why I left for a little bit, listen I promise you I won't take my problems out on you anymore," says Lisa as she wipes her tears from her eyes.

"Lisa where is we going once we leave here?." "Oh I'm sorry we can go back to your house" replies Lisa, "so the girls can see your mom, then I need to take Narlyn to see her mom so can you please keep an eye on Jymayia?" Asked Lisa.

Lisa pulled up to the building of Children and Youth, she gets out of the car, as she was walking around to take Narlyn out of her car seat she see's Nook pulling up with her nose turned up. Laughing Lisa just walks in the building as she hears Nook calling her daughter's name. Nook walks inside and walks right up to Lisa and gets in her face, "SO YOU DIDN'T HEAR ME CALLING MY DAUGHTER?!!!" yells Nook. Narlyn slides back behind Lisa's leg and peaks out to look at her mother. Lisa want to put her finger in Nooks face, but put it down once she saw the caseworker walk up.

"Is everything okay out here?," asked the caseworker, as she heard Nook being loud. Yes everything is fine responded Nook, I was just happy to see my daughter she replied. Nook reached out for Narlyn to take her hand, but Narlyn hesitated before grabbing her mother's hand. Lisa looked at Nook with this look and then looked at Narlyn. "Go ahead" says Lisa, "I will be right in the next room," she assured her step daughter. In Lisa's mind she is trying to figure out why Narlyn didn't want to go to her mother, the only time they see each other is when they are here at the Children and Youth office. As the visit was over Nook walks out of the office with the look of death on her face, she tells Lisa keep it up and you will be next, you will be in the grave next to your dead baby daddy. Lisa stands up but before she can go after Nook Narlyn comes out of the room and runs over to her and grabs her legs, she turns to look at her mom then turns away. Nook gives Lisa the finger and walks out of the building without telling her daughter bye.

As Lisa was about to question Narlyn the caseworker walks out of her office, "Lisa can I talk with you here in my office for a second?" says the caseworker. Lisa is looking at Narlyn and she is shaking. "Lisa," says the caseworker again, Lisa snaps out of her thoughts and walks into the office holding Narlyn in her arms. Lisa as speaking with Miss Williams a few minutes ago we are going to stop the visitations with her for 6 months. Miss Williams will need to take parenting classes before we allow Narlyn to be in her care again, and that is with a caseworker or without one.

"Can I ask what brought this on?" asked Lisa. The caseworker explains to Lisa that she see fear in the child and her job is to make sure that the child will be safe in the care of their mother and father. The caseworker goes on asking Lisa questions about if Narlyn sleeps at night, if she cries in her sleep. "Narlyn is happy when she is with me," explained Lisa, 'she sleeps all night when she is at home with me." The caseworker gave Lisa some papers to sign before they had wrapped up the visit.

On the way walking out of the building of the Children of Youth she sees Nook sitting in her car looking at her, as she sped pass Lisa she said your next so watch your back and drove off. Lisa wasn't scared of Nook but she didn't want to do anything stupid to jeopardize her having the custody of Narlyn.

As Lisa was driving off her phone rings and it was Bianca, should I answer this call thought Lisa. "Hello" says Lisa, "hey girl what you doing?" replies Bianca, "I'm having a cookout here at the house if you would like to come up with the girls?" she says. Now this girl just told me that her friend was pregnant by my man like 2 weeks ago and now she wants me to come to a cookout where I know that this girl is going to be at Lisa thinks to herself. "You know what?," says Lisa, "yes I will be there." "Is it okay if I bring someone with me?." Bianca got quit for second, "oh okay that's fine" she said, sure you can bring whoever you want to bring.

"Okay I will see you in 2 hours" replied Lisa as she hangs the phone up. Lisa calls Terri and tells her that she has to drive to Chester, she explains why and for Terri to be ready to go to the cook out when she gets back. Lisa has her own plans for Miss Bianca.

After Lisa picks up her girlfriend in Chester she heads back to Norristown to pick Terri and Jymayia up. On the way to Raheem's house, Lisa tells the ladies a little of what is going on, she didn't tell them everything just what she wants them to know. As they pulled up to the front gate, Bianca buzz them in the gate. Bianca's face turned a shade darker once she seen Terri get out of the car, but she played it kool. "Hey guys," says Bianca as she gave everyone a hug.

As the ladies went over toward the pool to sit down Lisa spotted Tina looking her direction with these dark sunglasses on. Lisa leans over to her girlfriend Dana, "there goes the chick that says she is pregnant by Jimmy." Now Dana and Lisa are child hood friends, they grow up in Chester together. When Lisa moved to Norristown the 1st person she met was Terri and then they became best of friends. But Dana and Lisa were just alike, they played no games when it came to fighting. But Lisa said, "that's not what we came here for," she tells Dana that she just wanted to point Bianca and Tina out, Lisa tells Dana before she gets her hands dirty she had to put the final pieces together and that's where Terri comes in at. But before Lisa does that she had to get some more information on Bianca and Tina.

Lisa walks over to where Tina was sitting and sits down beside Tina, with a serious look on her face, Lisa says, "so you're having a baby by my kid's father," as she leans back in the chair. Tina sits up and was about to get loud with Lisa, but Lisa said in a common voice, "sweetie don't get loud with me, because I will turn this party out," as she looked right into Tina eyes. Tina sat back in her chair, "Lisa, I don't know who told you that lie, but no I'm not pregnant by Jimmy" she says, "and just to let you know I'm glad he's dead, Lisa." "What that man did to me he deserved to die," says Tina.

Soon as she said that Lisa smacked Tina so hard that blood came out of her mouth, Lisa then got up and walked away, "I told you I will turn this party out Tina so don't ever disrespect my finace again" and Lisa walked away. Now no one saw what was going on over by where Tina and Lisa was sitting but Raheem. Tina got up holding her mouth and walked in the house, Bianca followed behind her.

"Hey girl! are you ok?" asked Bianca as she saw that Tina took a paper towel to wipe off her lip as it was still bleeding. Tina turned to look at her friend. Bianca asked "What happen?," "What! she punched you in your face?" asked Bianca. Tina just looked at Bianca, "no she slapped me," says Tina as she washed the blood off of her face. Raheem walks in the kitchen where the ladies were talking, "Bianca can I talk to you for a minute," he says.

As they walked into the other room Terri walks in the house, "oh hey I'm sorry I was looking to use the bathroom," she said. Bianca gave Terri this dirty look, "it's right over there" says Raheem. "Bianca, I heard and saw the whole thing with Tina and Lisa, B did Tina do anything to my brother cause she said to Lisa that she was glad that Jimmy was dead because of what he did to her, and you didn't tell me that Tina said she was pregnant by Jimmy. Heck "B" I didn't even know that they we're still messing with each other," says Raheem. With an attitude Bianca says, "yeah Raheem, that dog was still messing with my friend and yes she was pregnant by him but she got rid of the baby. Raheem, Jimmy was a dog and he was cheating on Lisa, I tried to tell Lisa that and she didn't believe me." snapped Bianca.

Raheem looked at his wife with this confused look on his face, "listen "B" I don't know if my brother and your girl Tina was messing with each other or not, Jimmy tells me everything "B" and I would think that he would have told me about Tina. I knew my brother couldn't stand her "B" and now you're telling me that he was still messing with her and got her pregnant." Raheem walked away from his wife, Bianca walks back in the kitchen with Tina.

Terri comes out of the bathroom with a slight smile on her face, she heard the whole conversation between Raheem and Bianca, but she didn't tell Lisa what was going on, Terri knew her best friend well enough that if she told her what was said that Lisa would turn that cookout upside down, so she didn't say a word.

CHAPTER FIVE

Lisa and her girls were leaving the cookout, on their way driving out the gate Lisa sees the same black truck riding past the gate. Is that the same truck she thinks to herself. Lisa, Lisa, says Terri, is everything okay she asked. Lisa snaps out of what she was thinking and turns back to look at her daughters, yeah everything is good she said as she made her turn to go back to Norristown.

On the drive back Lisa just kept looking in the rear view mirror making sure that this truck wasn't following her. "Lisa what's wrong asked Terri?." "Nothing, I just got some things on my mind that's all," she replied back. Lisa had to play it kool cause she didn't want her friends asking questions or to upset Narlyn. Narlyn was very smart and she picked up on a lot going on around her, so Lisa didn't want her to see that something was bothering her so Lisa sparked up a conversation with her friends just to ease her mind.

As Lisa and her friends pulled up to Jimmy's mother's house Nook rides pass, she pulls over at the corner of Marshall and Green and hopes out of the car to go into the Chinese Store. Lisa phone rings and it was an unknown number so Lisa didn't answer it, the same unknown number calls back but this time leaves a message.

Nook comes out of the store looks over where Lisa was and gets back into her car and speeds off. Lisa checks the message and it was Nook saying that she was going to make Lisa's life miserable like Jimmy made hers. She also said that she is coming to take her daughter back if she has to hurt Lisa as well. Now Lisa knows that Nook really wasn't going to do anything, Nook just had another baby a month ago and I know she didn't want to lose both of her kids. But Lisa just laughed at the message.

Lisa got her daughters together, she puts them in the car seats and was ready to head back to Chester, she hasn't stayed home since Raheem came to her house. Her and her girlfriend pulled up to her father's house laughing about the voicemail that she had received from Nook. As Lisa walked into her father's house her dad asked if he could talk to her, she said "okay let me put the girls down for bed then we can talk" she said to her dad.

Her father had this look on his face but Lisa didn't question the look. As she came back down the steps her dad was on the front porch talking with someone on the phone. Lisa sits down beside him and waits for him to get off of the phone. Once he hung up the phone he turned to his daughter, Lisa he says, he has this look in his eyes. "Dad what's going on?," she asked. "Lisa that was the Philadelphia Fire Dept and someone has set your house on fire," her father told her. Lisa puts her head down, she didn't cry she was more angry about the news her father just gave her.

"Are you alright?," her dad asked her as he puts his arms around his daughter to comfort her, Lisa tells her dad that, "everything will be alright," she also tells her dad about the voicemail that Nook left her when she was in Norristown dropping Terri off. She stands up and screams "WHERE IS ME

AND MY DAUGHTERS GOING TO LIVE AT NOW?!!! she picks up her phone and calls Nook but it went straight to voicemail. Lisa was going to leave a message but she thought to herself she had to play her cards right. If she comes at Nook in any kind of way she can lose Narlyn for good and she didn't want that. Lisa asked if the girls can stay there while she drives to Philly to see what was going on with her house.

As she pulls up to the house she sees Raheem standing there just looking. Lisa gets out and walks up to Raheem, "so how did you know that my house was on fire?" asked Lisa. "Bianca said that, it was a big fire in Philly, she showed me where it was and I looked at the address and saw that it was Jimmy's address so I came down to see if you and the kids were alright. Lisa listen I just want to help you, I feel like you have this trust issue with me, Jimmy is my brother and I am going to look out for you and his kids Raheem said with tears in his eyes. The same way you want to know who did this to Jimmy is the same way I want to know," says Raheem as he walked away. Lisa just stood there looking with tears in her eyes.

The Fire Chief walks over to Lisa and tells her that someone threw a fire boom into her house and that's what started the fire. Lisa just cried shaking her head wondering who would do this too her.

She gets into her car to head back to Chester but before she pulled off she called her dad to tell him what the Fire Cheif had told her. On her way driving back to her fathers house she was thinking about what Raheem had said to her, Lisa is still wondering why would Bianca tell him that a house was on fire and he knew that was Jimmy's house, something is not adding up Lisa thinks to herself.

She gets back to her dads house, her dad is sitting out on the porch, Lisa walks over to him and just falls in his arms crying, "dad why is someone trying to hurt us?, what was Jimmy really into?." Now Lisa was second guessing herself about who killed Jimmy.

The next morning Lisa wakes up asking her dad can he watch the girls why she make some runs, she needs to look for another house. Her father offered her to stay there with him, he was worried about his daughter with all that is going on. Now her father can help her with all of this but Lisa asked that he would stay out of it and let her handle it. Lisa had an ideal of who killed Jimmy but before she did anything or want to any cops she had to make sure that it was the right person. See Nook was the number 1 suspect in this but she has been having 2nd thoughts about it. Lisa really doesn't know Brick like that and she was wondering how he got her phone number. She knew that Jimmy wouldn't call her from no other man phone.

Tina she really not worried about right now, she's very unsure about Raheem too, she thinks this man calls Jimmy his brother but he was acting funny also. Now Lisa is in her car in deep thoughts where she was sitting at a light that turned green and then back to red 2 times. The car behind her horn was beeping over and over, Lisa finally snapped out of her thoughts and pulled off on a yellow light.

Lisa hoped on 476 on her way to Philly, she pulled up to the house that her and her family once lived in, she sat in the car with tears coming down her eyes. She was very upset at this point, she thinks 1st they take my man away from me, and now my house. She knew that she had to get to the bottom of this right away before things start to get real serious. Before she really had to get her dad involved and that she didn't want to do.

The Fire Chief and his crew was still there when Lisa pulled up, she finally got out of the car to go and talk with the Fire Chief. The house was burned to the ground almost, according to the Fire Dept it was arson. They questioned her about who would want to set the fire to her house, Lisa replied she really doesn't know.

After Lisa was done talking with the Police and the Fire Chief she took pictures and called her dad, Lisa cried to her dad asking why would someone want to set her house on fire. While Lisa was there Raheem pulled up. "Lisa I am sorry that this has happened to you and if you need a place to stay at until you and the girls find a place to go you can come to the house and stay, we have plenty of room," he said. Lisa just looked at Raheem, "no I'm okay I will figure this out," she says. "Okay I was just asking Lisa, trying to help my brother's girl out that's all," he said with base in his voice.

As Raheem was walking away he made a phone call, Lisa was trying to listen but couldn't hear what he was saying to the person on the phone. Lisa watched him pull off and then she made a call to Kyle. Lisa was very smooth with what she was doing and who she will trust, and right now she didn't trust nobody but her family.

"Hello," says Kyle, "hey Kyle can you meet me please at the Clock Bar?," she said. "Sure, is everything alright he asked". Lisa got quite for a second, "yes, everything is fine I just need to talk to you." Kyle asked if Lisa was in Philly and how long will it take for her to get there. Lisa replied "yes,

I'm in Philly I'm at the house and I will be there in 20 minutes." She said and hung the phone up. Lisa sat in her car thinking Kyle lives in Philly he would know what is going on before Raheem would know. Now it's time to get some answers Lisa said to herself as she sped off.

Lisa parked on Broad Street and walked over to Germantown Ave where she meant Kyle just getting out of his car. They both walked into the bar and sat at one of the booths. Kyle ordered drinks for the both of them. "Okay what's up with you?," asked Kyle, "you sounded kinda serious on the phone earlier." Lisa just looked at Kyle before she said anything, tears came to her eyes, "Kyle someone set my house on fire, and as I was there Raheem pulled up which was very weird to me that he came all the way from his house and you're right here in Philly and didn't even know that the house was on fire. Kyle, can I ask you a question? How much do you know about Raheem?," asked Lisa. "Do you think that he would do anything to hurt Jimmy?."

"Lisa, Jimmy and Raheem are like brothers, I really don't think that he would do anything to him let alone kill him," replied Kyle. "Where are you going with all of this?," asked Kyle. 'Why would you think that he would kill Jimmy?." Lisa thought about her answers before she said anything. She really didn't want Kyle to know all that was going on with Raheem showing up at the house a couple of times unannounced. She didn't want him to know that she knew Bianca was from Norristown.

"Kyle I don't know he has got very strange since Jimmy been going and it's freaking me out," says Lisa. "Lisa listen Raheem probably was already in Philly because he has family here and that's why he got to your house so quick." 'He did say Bianca called him and told him that Jimmy house was on fire, and that she saw it on the citizen app page," says Lisa. "Listen I wouldn't worry about Raheem if I was you, I just think since that's Jimmy right hand man he just wants to make sure that your good. Besides that's what Jimmy would have wanted is for all of us to make sure you and the kids are good."

"But Kyle I don't hear from you as much as I hear from Raheem." "Lisa, if you don't call me I know that you're alright. Look Lisa I know that Raheem has nothing to do with my cousin's death. Jimmy had a lot of people that hated him out there in the streets, he knew one day that they were going to come after him that's why he was trying to get out of the game. Lisa, my cousin tried his hardest to keep you and his children out of harms way, Jimmy fell in love with you from the day he met you but you was too young for him. We knew that he wanted to marry you before you knew it Lisa, Raheem was his best man, so why would he want to kill him," says Kyle.

Lisa looked into Kyle eyes to see if there was any trust for her to believe him. "Okay Kyle, I'm a take your word that this man has nothing to do with Jimmy's death. Kyle just to let you know if I ever find out who did this to him it's over for them and I mean that from the bottom of my heart," says Lisa as she picked up here drink to drink it.

After Lisa and Kyle had a couple of drinks she told Kyle that she had to go and pick the kids up from her sister house, she also told Kyle that they were staying in a hotel until she has found another house to move into. Lisa didn't want anyone to know her moves and where she was going to move to. Lisa still doesn't trust no one but her father. Her own sisters really doesn't even know the story of what is going on in there little sister life right know. Lisa feels the less they know the better off they will be, Lisa doesn't like people to ask questions and she knew that would be actually what her sisters would do was ask a lot of questions.

Kyle walks Lisa to her car, "please tell Mimi I said hi and we will catch up with each other after this is all over," says Lisa. "No problem," says Kyle as he turns to walk to his car. After he watches Lisa pull off, he called Raheem to ask him what was going on with him. "Man you in Philly?," Kyle asked Raheem. Raheem replied back to Kyle with a "yeah I'm here in Philly visiting my people over on the west side, why what's up?." "Nothing, I was asking cause I just was with Lisa and she said that you came to the house while she was there talking with the cops and the fire department and I just wanted to know if you was still in Philly so we can go get a drink or something."

Raheem got quite for a second, "hey little brother I'm on my way back home right now, Bianca called talking about something was going on with my son so I'm on my way there to see what was going on with him. So I'm catch up with you some other time when I'm back in Philly," said Raheem. Kyle felt something fishy with that conversation, but still said, "okay that's all good we will catch up another time, 1 my brother I will get at you," said Raheem and then hung the phone up.

Now Kyle knows Raheem well and he knows that Raheem loved his cousin Jimmy and doesn't want to think nothing different about him, but Kyle got a bad vibe from the conversation he just had with him. Kyle shook it off and kept it in the back of his mind, he didn't say anything to Lisa cause like Lisa now Kyle is wondering if Raheem had anything to do with the murder of his big cousin/ big brother. Kyle didn't play when it came to his family, he will make sure no one is left in your family after he was done.

On Kyle's drive back home all he can think about was the conversation he had with Lisa, then the conversation he had with Raheem. When he got home his twin sister Kayla was sitting outside. "Hey twin what's up?," she said. Kyle looked at her with this confused look on his face. Kayla knew something was wrong, so she asked her twin brother what was going on. Kyle and Kayla were very close, Kyle sat down beside her and confined in his twin sister what he heard from Lisa and from Raheem.

"Kyle do you think Raheem would do something like that to Jimmy?," asked Kayla. "Sis I don't know, I mean you know the situation that happen years ago and Raheem might be still upset about that," says Kyle. "Yeah but Jimmy didn't know about that until after Raheem introduced her to him and Jimmy left her alone after that. Besides they always shared girls growing up and it wasn't a problem," says Kyle, but Kyle really had a bad feeling about this.

Kayla please don't say anything to Lisa or Mimi about our conversation I will take care of it says Kyle as he got up and walked into the house.

CHAPTER SIX

Lisa found her and her daughters a 4 bedroom house in Northeast Philadelphia, Lisa had to buy all new things for her and her daughters due to everything she owned was burned to the ground in the fire. No one knew where she moved, only her family knew and that's the way she was going to keep it until she got to the bottom of who killed Jimmy. Lisa had all new furniture moved in as soon as possible so her and the girls can move in right away. After everything was moved in and everything was setup the way Lisa wanted it she laid down on the sofa and took a nap. As she was sleeping her phone was ringing off the hook. HELLO! HELLO! Says Lisa, no one said anything on the other end, Lisa looks at her phone half asleep still and the call came from an unknown number.

She laid the phone back down and tried to go back to sleep, ding ding Lisa looked at her phone again and it was a voice message left on her phone. Lisa listen to the message and it was a females voice saying that the next time she thinks about coming at her again she will think twice.

Lisa sat up thinking, now she knew what Nook's voice sounded like so she knew it wasn't her leaving the message. She thinks to herself the only other person that she had a problem with was Tina and she knew that Tina didn't have her number. Lisa laid back down thinking about the message that was left on her answering machine, thinking to herself who's voice could it have been.

Ring, Ring, this time the number appeared on her phone, Lisa answered the phone, the caller on the end started laughing, "Hello," said Lisa, "who is this, please stop playing on my phone," she says then hung up the phone. Lisa *67 the number back, the phone was ringing and a female answered the phone, at first Lisa didn't say anything. "Hello," the person on the line said, Lisa still didn't respond cause she was trying to see if she can catch the voice.

The voice sounded like Bianca's voice but it wasn't Bianca's phone number, so Lisa called Bianca just to see what she was doing and just to confirm the voice that was left on her answering machine.

Ring Ring, Bianca answered her phone, "Hello" she said, "hey Bianca" says Lisa, "hey girl" responded Bianca, "what's up?" "Nothing really" says Lisa as she tries to keep her on the phone so she can make sure that the voice was the same. As they talked for a little bit Lisa realized that the caller on the message was Bianca's voice. "Girl I was just sitting her trying to figure out who and why someone is playing on my phone, they keep calling breathing hard and laughing real loud in my ear." Bianca was quite for a second, then she responded, "Lisa could it have been the wrong number, people do call the wrong number or they just like playing on peoples phones, it probably was some kids just playing around," says Bianca.

"Yeah you right Bianca I'm tripping I need to chill out with all of this thinking someone is out to get me," says Lisa as she waits for a response from Bianca. But Bianca didn't make any comments back, she just said to

Lisa, "girl you sound like you are tired, was you sleeping?." Lisa didn't say anything at first, Lisa cleared her throat and responded, "yes, I was asleep until people started playing on my phone." "Bianca I'm a have to call you back later I need to rest my head a little it hurts," "oh okay girl call me later."

After Lisa got off the phone with Bianca she called Terri, Terri picked up on the 1st ring, "hey Lisa what's up? Is everything alright she questioned?." Now Lisa know that Terri would never do anything to hurt her but she didn't rule her out of her playing on her phone. But the voice wasn't her best friend's voice, Lisa puts her head down and said to herself am I tripping cause now I'm thinking that my best friend would betray me.

"Lisa! Is you there says Terri?." "Yeah I'm here Terri, my head is just hurting that's all," says Lisa. "Terri someone has been playing on my phone for hours, they would call and don't say nothing, then they called left a message telling me that I played with the wrong person that if I come at them again I was going to get it." "Wow this is getting out of hand Lisa, I think you need to call the detectives and tell them that you have been getting calls and that someone is threatening you. Lisa you can't keep allowing this to go on your going to get yourself hurt," says Terri with fear in her voice.

"Yeah you're right Terri I will call the detective tomorrow, I will show him all the messages and let him hear the voice messages." "Wait! Lisa they have been sending you messages too, I'm calling Kyle right now," says Terri. "Wait Terri please don't call Kyle, I spoke with Kyle the other day about this and he said that him and Raheem was going to take care of everything." But Terri, then Lisa got quite. "Hello Lisa are you there?," says Terri. "Yes I'm here," says Lisa with a low voice. "Terri I'm not sure if I trust Raheem, I don't know Raheem like you'll do, this man puts a bad taste in my mouth Terri. He showed up at my house when the fire happened Terri," says Lisa as she starts to cry.

"Lisa what do you mean he showed up at your house, how? Lisa how did Raheem know that there was a fire at your house?," asked Terri. "Exactly" says Lisa, "he lives an 1/2 hour away Terri but he jumps out of the car and runs over to me asking was I okay. I just looked at him thinking how he knew but Kyle, Mimi or anyone else in your family didn't know and they live in Philly," says Lisa."Terri he said that Bianca has citizen app on her phone and my address came up and that's how he knew that the house was on fire. Get this Terri, I asked him how did he get here so quick he said that he was already in Philly at someone's house when Bianca called him. Terri I really don't trust this man," says Lisa. "Kyle told me I was tripping that Raheem and Jimmy were like brothers and that he really don't think that Raheem would do anything to hurt Jimmy."

"Lisa they were very close, I mean they did everything together, I really don't think Raheem had anything to do with my brother's murder. I'm like Kyle, I think you're making a mistake with this girl," says Terri. "Okay I may be tripping and I will leave it alone," says Lisa, "but just the way Raheem is moving is what's making me think otherwise Terri, but I'm a give up on that and move on, I will let the detectives handle it." "Listen, I got to go," says Lisa, "I will hit you back later," she says before they end the conversation.

Lisa got up from her nap, got herself together so she can go and pick the girls up from her dad's house. On her way leaving out of Philly she stops by the old house, Lisa sat there in her car just looking, she turned to look and when she seen the same black truck drive past her. Lisa is looking like this can't be the same truck she thinks, this time Lisa says to herself that she's going to take a picture of the licenses plate so if she was to see that truck again she will know that it was the same truck that she seen in Norristown. As the truck drove slowly pass her she puts her head down so the driver wouldn't see her looking.

Lisa snapped a picture of the plate on the truck and waited until the truck was out of site before she pulled off. Lisa knew she was playing a dangerous game by trying to be a detective herself but she knew that she had to get to the bottom of this cause she knows that the detectives are not doing their jobs because she hasn't heard anything from them in over 2 months. Each time she calls to see where they are at with the case they lie and tell her that they are still working on the case and they have no leads at this point. Lisa knew that was a lie, Lisa knew that Norristown police department didn't like Jimmy from what he has told her.

Lisa calls her dad and asked if he can run a plate for her and to get back to her with who the owner of this black truck is. Lisa jumps on the highway heading to Chester to pick up the girls and take them to see their new home, she also thought that she will pick Terri up too so they can sit and talk. Lisa needed to know really how close Raheem and Jimmy really was.

When Lisa got to Chester she sees that she had a missed call on her phone but didn't hear her phone ring, the miss call was from Nook, Lisa look and said to herself why is she calling me and what does this girl want, she didn't leave message or anything. Nook calls again and this time Lisa answered the phone, "Hello" she says. "Little girl you forgot that I was suppose to see my daughter today," says Nook. Lisa thinks to herself, wait Nook has no more visits with Narlyn for another 6 months, so why is she calling me. "Nook you already know that you don't have visits with Narlyn anymore, you lost your rights to see her," Lisa says.

Lisa looked at her watch after the call she just had with Nook Lisa then calls the social worker to tell her that Nook called her thinking that she had a visit today with Narlyn. The caseworker told Lisa that she will give Nook a call and talk with about the case.

Lisa gets to her father house to get the girls, her dad called her to come into his office that he needed to talk to her, her father hands a letter that was from someone he knew in Philadelphia County Police Department. "What's this?," asked Lisa. "It's a letter saying that your house was set on fire purposely and that there was a fire bomb that was throwing through the window. They have a video showing someone dressed in all black running up to your house and throwing the bomb into the window and running off down the street. They don't have footage on which way the person ran after they left from the site of the camera that was on your block. They didn't even see what type of car they ran to. Lisa I think that you should move out here with me just until this is all over with," says Lisa's father.

Lisa just stood there looking at the letter thinking why is someone out to get her? What was Jimmy really into that he never to her? Lisa thinks. She calls Kyle and tells him about the letter, "Hey Kyle was Jimmy into anything else other than hustling in the streets?," asked Lisa.

"Lisa you know being big like Jimmy was going to be people that will be jealous of him right," says Kyle. "We all got into to some things Lisa, they hated Jimmy for sleeping with their girls, the chicks hated Jimmy for hurting their feelings. I'm not going to say that my cousin was a good or bad guy Lisa, he was just being himself Lisa, he never had a girl that he was in a serious relationship with so he did him. He was a big time drug dealer in these streets and that you already know, so it could've been anyone that killed my cousin and set his house on fire Lisa.

"Jimmy had enemies here in Philly, Norristown, Jersey, New York, he had them all over Lisa. My cousin sold drugs where he wanted to and didn't care Lisa, he made money all over that was just what he did. He also had a lot friends in these places as well that really was good to him too because they see that he was a man about his money. See Lisa, Jimmy was like his father, his dad made money all over this world and had a lot of woman too. Once his dad got into construction and wanted to get out of the game, his dad ended up having his own business but he got killed right after all of that. Lisa I know that you're worried about you and the girls that your fearful of what would happen to you'll, this is why I tell you over and over to keep in contact with us Lisa," says Kyle.

"I hear you Kyle, my father wants the girls and I to move back to Chester with him until everything dies down. I moved to a place where no one knows where I'm at," says Lisa. "Kyle I don't know but my gut feeling is that I don't trust the fact that Raheem came to the seen that quick Kyle, I know you say that he's like a brother to you'll but until I feel comfortable around him I really don't trust him," says Lisa.

"Lisa I will check into why Raheem was in Philly at that time, trust me, my family will find out if Raheem had anything to do with this, don't worry we will find out what's going on. So Lisa just call me if you need anything and remember I am here for you if you and the girls need anything or even if you just need to talk," responded Kyle.

After Lisa hung the phone up from speaking with Kyle she told her dad that she was going into Norristown to see Terri. As Lisa got on the highway to go see her best friend she kept thinking about Raheem and how he just showed up at the house after the fire, and when she gave him a hug how he was trying to pull her close to him. I really don't trust this man Lisa said to herself, What is he up too? And, Why did Brick call my phone? How did he even get my phone number? Lisa is saying to herself out loud. I know Jimmy would never give any of his friends my phone number.

Lisa pulls up to Jimmy's mother's house, as she's sitting there in the car she notices the same black truck with tinted windows slowly riding down the street pass her. The truck stops at the corner and sits there for a few minutes then turns to go down Marshall toward Arch. Lisa quickly gets out of the car she takes the girls out of their car seats, she goes into the house and calls for Terri. Jimmy's mother comes down the steps and sees Lisa peeking out of the window. "Is everything alright Lisa?," asked Jimmy's mother, she kinda scared Lisa when she said that, Lisa turns and says "yes everything is fine, I was trying to see if the car that is parking out here was going to hit my car," lies Lisa as she walks away from the window.

Terri comes down and as she was walking down the steps her mom was walking up the steps with the girls going into her bedroom. "Hey girl what's up?," asked Terri. Lisa looks at her best friend, "Terri I need to talk with you, remember the day I went to get my other car from the dealer," "yes, I remember," said Terri. Lisa gets quite, she really didn't want to sound like she was crazy by saying what she was about to say. 'Terri I think someone is watching me," she says looking at Terri with a tear in her eye, "I know it sounds crazy Terri, but it's this black truck that was following us that day. That is why I told you to drive around the block and park at the corner of Marshall and Arch. Terri I brought me a gun says Lisa as she is looking at her best friend."

"I fear that my life is in danger Terri, you may think that I am crazy but I know that my house was set on fire and here are the papers that my dad gave me. I have been getting calls telling me that I am next, Raheem showed up at my house twice Terri. The one night I was at his house about to spend the night there with Bianca and the kids but Bianca and I got into an argument so I left. When I got home Raheem was standing in the driveway when I pulled up. I asked him why was he there and he said that there was someone at my door and that the neighbor called him. I asked why didn't the neighbor call me, and Raheem's response was that the man did call me but I didn't answer the phone."

"But Terri he didn't call me and when I questioned it to my neighbor he said he was drinking that night and doesn't remember calling anyone cause he didn't hear my alarm go off in the house or see anyone knocking on the door. Besides, Terri the alarm people would have called me if the alarm was going off. Then for Raheem to show up the night of the fire Terri, this man lives an ½ hour away from Philly, but he said that he was already down there and that he got a call from Bianca stating that she saw that there was on fire and that she seen it on citizens app."

"Terri it doesn't make sense to me and get this his brother Brick whatever he is to Raheem calls my phone from a private number, then going to say that Jimmy used his phone the one day to call me that is how he got my number when I asked him how he got my phone number."

"Then this chick Nook is really going to make me go upside her head but for the sake of her daughter I just try to ignore her. And Tina, when I asked her at the cookout was she pregnant she said that it was a lie that she never told Bianca that she was having a baby by Jimmy. Terri now you see why I can't trust anyone right now, yes I maybe tripping but I know I'm not says Lisa. Lisa reaches into her pocketbook and grabs the earring that she found up there by the Pizza Shop, she wanted to show Terri it but she just put it back in her purse and figured that she will save that detail for later."

CHAPTER SEVEN

After Lisa spent over 2 hours talking with her best friend she decides that she will take a trip just her and the girls, Lisa knew that the court case for Narlyn and her mother wasn't for another 3 months so she told Terri that she was going to Jamaica for 2 weeks and that she was going to turn her phone off so she can clear her head from all that is going on. Lisa wanted so much to fill her best friend in with all the details that she has but everyone thinks that she is going crazy. At some point Lisa thinks that she is also going crazy too, but she knows in her heart that she's not going crazy. Lisa needs to find out more on Raheem and Brick and her father is the right person to find out that information.

"Hello,' answered Lisa's father. Lisa explained to her dad all that she needs him to do. Lisa also told her dad that she was going away for 2 weeks and that her phone will be off for those 2 weeks and that she will call him twice a week to see what he has found out on the 2 men.

"Terri I will also call you to let you know that I made it to my destination, I will call Kyle while I am there but I will not tell him where I am at, and Terri please don't tell anyone that I am going if someone asks you. Just say that I am spending time with my family in Chester," says Lisa.

Lisa and Terri goes and sit outside and as they were walking out of the door Lisa spots the black truck parked on the corner across from the Chinese store. She stops but she really didn't want Terri to know why she stop, she looks down and says why my sandal get stock she laughs to Terri as she was looking out the door. But she knew that Terri would ask questions so Lisa just walked out of the door and sat down, Lisa put her shades on and kept looking down the street at the black truck.

Here comes Nook and her friends again riding past laughing, but when Lisa looked down on the corner of Marshall and Green to see if the truck was still there the truck had already pulled off. I wonder if that is the detectives watching me thinks Lisa, she puts the black truck out of her mind cause now she thinks that it is the detective and she doesn't went to blow their cover, so Lisa was at ease now and it kind a took a lot of her thoughts away knowing that she was safe by this black truck.

Lisa got a call from Bianca, "hey girl, what's up?," asked Lisa, "hey I was wondering if you seen Raheem?," Lisa didn't say anything at first, Lisa was just wondering why Bianca was calling her and asking her have she seen her man and why would Lisa see him. "Bianca, why would I see Raheem?," asked Lisa, was he supposed to come and see me about something. "No, Lisa I asked because Nook called him last night and they were talking for a while on the phone, I was easy dropping on their conversation and I heard him say that he was going to talk to you about something." "Bianca I haven't seen or heard anything from Raheem and if he was to come to me about Nook I would have told him I didn't want to hear it," say Lisa. "Okay" says Bianca, "I was just checking to see if he called you."

After they hung up Lisa looked at Terri and said this call was weird, Lisa goes on to tell Terri what the call was about, Terri just looked at Lisa thinking to herself what was Bianca up too. Lisa and her best friend just laughed and continue on with their conversation they were having before Bianca called. Lisa phone rings again and this time it was Nook calling, Lisa answered the call and to her surprise Nook asked if she can talk to Lisa alone and if Lisa can come to her house. Lisa told her that wouldn't be a good ideal and that if Nook wanted to talk with her that she would have to do it around the social worker and that she wasn't coming to her house.

Nook says "okay," and that she assured Lisa that she wasn't on that type of time that she thought because Lisa had her daughter that they needed to become friends instead of enemies. Lisa snapped! "Nook you just drove past me laughing with your friends, you kept telling me how I was going to be laying next to my dead baby father like Jimmy wasn't your daughter father as well. What is it that you need to say to me? Nook" says Lisa as she was getting upset that Nook even called her phone with this.

Nook laughed a little before she went on to say, "Lisa Jimmy loved me as well as he loved you, he really didn't want you to know that we still had dealings with each other, and to be honest with you Lisa my other daughter might be Jimmy's baby laughed Nook. I called Raheem to see how I can tell you all of this without getting into something with you." Lisa said in the commonest voice that, "she can, Nook I don't care what you and Jimmy had going on when he was here, I don't care if that baby is his either, what I really want is that you not call my phone again is that clear Nook?," says Lisa as she hung up the phone.

Lisa called Raheem and laid into him, after Lisa was done Raheem explained to Lisa that, "Nook was lying and that she wanted to talk to Lisa about seeing her daughter Narlyn without going through the caseworker. Lisa I said that she would have to talk to you, I didn't understand why she called me with the mess Lisa and how she got my number either. Nook has never said anything to me even when we were at the party in OD Park, she always use to just look at me and roll her eyes, so I was confused that she even called me," says Raheem. "Raheem, I don't want this girl calling me, I'm tired of her and your wife." "What does Bianca have to do with this, Lisa?." "Oh so your wife didn't tell you that she called me telling me that Tina was pregnant with Jimmy's baby and that she got rid of it. And that Tina was with Jimmy the night he got killed, they we're at some hotel that night?," says Lisa.

"Lisa, Jimmy wasn't with Tina that night, Tina was at my house with Bianca, they were there drinking getting drunk. Jimmy was in Philly and came to Norristown to meet someone for a drop off." "Raheem I know he was going to take his gun with him but I took it out of the car," cried Lisa. "Wait a minute, Lisa, that night Jimmy felt that the conversation with his client was fishy, he called me and said that some guy name Kenny asked for him to meet him at the Pizza Shop on Dekalb Street, but when Jimmy got there he didn't see Kenny out there."

"Lisa we were on the phone talking for 10 minute before Jimmy said he wasn't going to wait for Kenny much longer and that he was about to leave. I thought he had made the drop off, then 2 hours later I get the call that my brother is going," says Raheem. "Lisa I got to go I need to know what Bianca knows about the death of my little brother," replies Raheem as he wipes the tears from his eyes. Lisa was quite on the other end of the phone, "Raheem do you think Bianca know something about this?, cause her and Tina has been playing on my phone. I called Bianca out about it and she said that it wasn't her but it's her voice on my answering machine," says Lisa, "it was her playing on my phone Raheem," says Lisa.

"Listen, I am going to get to the bottom of this Lisa" replied Raheem, "trust me, she may be the mother of my kids but if she has anything to do with my brother getting killed Lisa then she has to go," says Raheem as he hung the phone up. Lisa turned and looked at Terri, "Lisa is everything okay?" asked Terri. Lisa sat there for a second before she respond to her best friend. "Terri, I think Bianca knows more then what she was telling me about Jimmy." "Raheem said that Jimmy came up here to do a drop off but the person never showed up, and he thinks that Bianca knows about it, and that he was listening to her and Nook's conversation. Terri what is going on?, asked Lisa to her best friend.

"There is a lot that you're not telling me about Bianca, you told me that she was from Norristown and that she was our age." Lisa looked at Terri and yelled! "TELL ME WHAT IS GOING ON IF YOU SAY THAT YOUR MY BEST FRIEND!, Terri turned and looked at Lisa, but before she could tell her what was going on Lisa phone rings and it was her father on the other end.

"Hey dad what's up?" "Lisa where are you?," he said. 'I'm here at Jimmy's mom's house with Terri." "Lisa I got the information that you asked me for, The guy Brick real name is Thomas Williams, he has a long list on his criminal record. He did time for a murder back in 2001 but he beat the case Lisa. And as far as Raheem he is clean he only have drug charges on his record and he did a bid for 2 years and the rest was probation." "Thank you dad," says Lisa as she got up to walk away from Terri. "Dad can you do me another favor?, I have 3 more names I need you to do a check on, I think Nook and Raheem's baby mother Bianca is related but I'm not for sure."

"Something just doesn't add up dad and I'm going to get it all out of Terri," says Lisa as she tells her dad that she will talk to him later. Lisa walks back over to Terri, "now is you going to tell me what is going on best friend?." 'Lisa I thought Jimmy would have told you everything by now," "What do you mean Terri everything. Terri listen I am racking my brain trying to find out what happened to Jimmy my daughter father, your brother so do you want to tell me what is going on or what?."

"Bianca and Nook are related, they're first cousins, Tina I don't know so much about, just that her and Bianca are close friends and that's all I know. Jimmy slept with Bianca first before her and Raheem met. Bianca played a joke on Jimmy telling her cousin to mess with him cause he had money," explains Terri.   "So, you as my best friend felt that you should hold all this information back for what Terri?," yelled Lisa. "Lisa listen you were going through a lot and I know how your temper is and I didn't went you to react to any of this, Lisa I'm sorry I really thought Jimmy told you what was going on. I knew my brother loved you a lot and I know my brother and how he felt about you."

"Terri it's not your fault, I know you was just looking out for me, but please don't hold things back from me like this again," says Lisa as she gave her best friend a hug. Lisa sat just looking at her best friend thinking about what she just heard. Lisa began putting the pieces together.

"Terri, so did Jimmy and Bianca ever mess with each other?," asked Lisa. Terri thought about the question before she answered it. "Lisa, Jimmy told me that Nook and Bianca placed a bet to see who would get Jimmy first. Jimmy played the both of them and slept with them both all because they played this joke on him. He told me that Bianca came at him first they slept with each other one time. But when Nook came at him he refused her at first. Lisa Jimmy was playing the game that they wanted to play."

"Okay, so what does Tina have to do with all of this? What part does she play in this?, asked Lisa. "Bianca put her in the bet Jimmy told me. Well was Jimmy and Tina in a relationship?," asked Lisa as she was trying to figure this whole thing out. "No they were just sleeping with each other and the only reason Jimmy was with Tina more was to make Bianca jealous because he knew that Bianca planned the whole thing between Nook, Tina and her."

"Once Jimmy saw that Bianca started acting different with Tina that's when he stopped messing with Tina, he laughed at the both of them because they played themselves he said, he said that they tried to play a player but got played. So Bianca thought if she started messing with his right hand man which is Raheem that Jimmy would get upset. But Jimmy didn't care that she was messing with Raheem." "Did Raheem know that Jimmy and Bianca slept with each other?" asked Lisa. "Yeah he knew, they were best friends Lisa, more like brothers, they told each other everything." "So why did Raheem wife her if he knew that she was doing this as a joke, it's not making any sense to me Terri," says Lisa. "Lisa I really don't know so I can't answer that question." "Okay so the day of the party at OD Park I saw Nook there all up on Jimmy, was they messing with each then asked Lisa?" "No they hadn't done anything with each other yet."

"Lisa his focus was on you, he told me a head of time to ask you to come to the party. Jimmy knew that you was a young buck but he said that he liked looking at you and that one day he was going to make you his girl, his wife. Lisa when we walked into that park Jimmy whole attention was on you and Nook saw that, and Jimmy walked away from her to come over to us and started talking to you."

"So Terri was I part of Jimmy's plan to get Nook jealous asked Lisa?" Terri laughed, "no my brother really wanted you, and if you wasn't younger than him you was going to be his girl that night." Terri and Lisa laughed, "so this explains why Bianca looked at my daughter the way she did when we were at her house. I took Jymayia out of her stroller and you should have seen the look on Bianca's face, she looked like she saw a ghost Terri. I asked her if everything was alright and she started stuttering saying how much Jymayia looked like Jimmy."

"Lisa, Bianca was in love with Jimmy also since the 1st day she saw him, they tried to hang out around my house when we were younger but Jimmy was never home he was always in Philly with Kyle and Raheem. When your party was at the OD Park that night Bianca and Raheem was starting to get into a relationship. I notice that Bianca and Nook really didn't say much to each other. Terri laughed and said because Nook was mad at her cousin. Why because he slept with Bianca 1st," laughed Lisa. "Terri these females is stupid," says Lisa.

CHAPTER EIGHT

As Lisa left her best friend on her way driving home she started thinking if Raheem knew that Jimmy and Bianca slept with each other why would he stay in a relationship with her knowing that this girl tried to set his right hand man up. This still doesn't add up to me she thinks to herself, and I am going to get to the bottom of all of this.

Ring Ring, "Hello" says Lisa, "hey baby girl it's your father," "hey dad what's up?" She asked. 'So I got all the information you asked for." "Dad, I got all I needed to know from Terri. Terri explained everything to me, now I just have to put all the pieces together," says Lisa. Her dad was quite for a second, "Lisa I hope that you're not thinking of doing anything stupid, I hope once you figure things out that you will go to the police and not handle it yourself." "Daddy I will be fine," she said with her voice cracking.

"Baby girl is you okay?" asked her father "Yes dad, I'm okay," says Lisa as she wipes the tears away from her eyes. "Dad I will call you later, the girls are in the car with me so I really can't talk." "Okay, please call me once you get in the house, Lisa I love you and please whatever information you have let me or the police handle it." Lisa tells her dad, "okay," and then hangs up the phone.   Once Lisa gets home she feeds the girls, she just sat there looking at Jymayia thinking about Jimmy. After she put the girls to bed she just laid on the sofa crying asking herself why would his right hand man want to hurt his best friend. Lisa said to herself that she was going to get to the bottom of this.

Lisa fell asleep on the sofa when her phone rings and it was Bianca, Lisa looks at the phone, why is this girl calling me this time of the night she thinks to herself. "Hello," says Lisa with her lip turned up, like why is this girl calling me. "Hey Lisa" says Bianca, Bianca starts crying on the phone telling Lisa that Raheem left her, that he has packed all of his clothes and all of his belongs. "Lisa I think that he has moved in with his other baby momma."

Lisa didn't say a word, she just sat there still thinking so why must she tell me what is going on in her life with her man like I really care. Lisa really wanted to asked Bianca why she didn't tell her that her and Nook were cousins, and why they played a trick on her man and now he is dead.

"Bianca what happen, why did he leave like that?," asked Lisa, like she really cared. Bianca cleared her throat before she answered the question. "Lisa is it possible that I can talk to you in person about this?" Lisa looked at her phone thinking why does she want to talk to me in person? What does this girl have up her sleeve?. "Um okay sure when would you like for me to come up there?," says Lisa.

"Is it possible that you can come this weekend if you don't mind?," Bianca replies. "Okay I will see you this weekend," says Lisa, after the conversation was over Lisa hung the phone up, she sat up on the sofa thinking why would Bianca want to talk to me about Raheem leaving her when she can easily talk to her best friend Tina about it? What is this girl doing? Lisa thinks.

The next morning Lisa calls Terri and tells her that Bianca called her and wanted her to come to her house this weekend coming. "Why does she want to talk to you? And I thought you'll really wasn't talking to each other like that?," says Terri. "Terri that's the thing we wasn't, I'm confused on why she even called me. She goes into telling me that Raheem took all of his belongings and left. So when I asked what happen that's when she said that she wanted to talk to me in person. Terri something doesn't sound right to me, cause why she couldn't just tell me on the phone."

"Girl what you think?" asked Lisa, Terri started laughing like as to say Lisa made a joke out of this. But little do Terri know Lisa wasn't laughing. Lisa wanted answers and now was the time to ask Bianca once she goes to see her. Lisa didn't care that Bianca and Raheem broke up, Lisa thought to herself that wasn't her problem. But all that Terri told her about the little tricks and games that was played and ended up causing her daughter father to lose his life was what was on her mind.

"Terri I have to go, I will give you a call back later, okay," says Lisa. After the ladies hung up from each other Lisa called Kyle. "Hello" answered Kyle, "Hey Kyle I need to talk with you about something." Lisa runs the whole thing down to Kyle about what she was going to do once she goes to visit Bianca. Lisa wants answers and she needs Kyle's help to get the answers that she is looking for. Lisa explains to Kyle that she wants him on standby just in case Bianca is trying to set her up. Kyle agrees with the plan.

After the call with Lisa Kyle makes a call to Raheem, he didn't say anything to Raheem about what Lisa told him, Kyle tells Raheem that he was calling to check up on him and to see if he wanted to go out tonight with him to have a drink. Raheem answered the phone with a low voice, "hey man what's up?," he says to Kyle. "Hey I'm going down to the Clock Bar later tonight and wanted to know if you're in Philly later would you like to join me?," asked Kyle.

Raheem other baby mother moved to Philly a couple of months ago so Kyle knew that Raheem would be in Philly. Kyle also knew if him and Bianca had it out and he took all of his things that he was coming to Philly to go to her house and stay. Raheem agreed to meet Kyle at the Clock Bar later on tonight. Once Kyle hung the phone up with Raheem he called Lisa back to tell her that the plan was in place. So later on that night the two men meant up at the bar so they can talk, Kyle was already in the bar waiting on Raheem to walk in.

Raheem comes in with this serious look on his face, he spots Kyle sitting at the bar, they moved from the bar to one of the booths in the back of the bar by the bathroom. Kyle asked Raheem was he okay, Raheem goes into telling Kyle about what happen with him and Bianca, how he didn't trust her anymore, how he knew that she was holding back something from him but he didn't know what it was. Raheem had this confused look on his face. He never once looked Kyle in the eyes.

Raheem looked like he had a lot on his mind, so Kyle asked again, "man what's up?, did you do something? Did you put your hands on her or something?" Raheem shook his head no but still had the confused look on his face. Kyle asked Raheem, "what was the fight about?," and that's when Raheem finally lifted his head up to look Kyle in the eyes. "Man I got to go," says Raheem as he hurried up and walked out the door, jumped in his car and pulled off.   Kyle called Lisa and told her that Raheem was acting weird like as if he did something to Bianca.

"Lisa I was talking to him and his mind was somewhere else, but once I asked what the fight was about that's when he finally lifted up his head and just looked at me, then he said he had to go." Lisa sat there in her own thoughts, she finally said, "Kyle I wonder what is going on?, why Bianca just couldn't tell me what was going on over the phone?, why does she went me to come to her house this weekend?. Kyle something not right, I feel it in my gutt that something isn't right."

"Yes I'm thinking the same thing," says Kyle, "Lisa do you think that he did something bad to her? Was he there when she called you?" "Kyle she said that he took all of his things and left, she was crying hysterically. Listen I am going to go up there tomorrow but I'm not going without my protection." replies Lisa.

"Wait! What kind of protection you talking about?, asked Kyle. Lisa goes to explain how this black truck with tinted windows was following her, and that's why she switched her car out. Kyle like the truck followed Terri and I for like 2 hours. I thought it was Nook riding in another car but it wasn't her because she drove past us in her car laughing at us. Then I haven't seen the truck for a couple days, then next thing you know Terri and I was sitting out in front of her house and the truck drove down the street and parked on the corn of Green and Marshall Street. I never told Terri that we were being followed are anything because I didn't want her to ask questions. But Kyle when I moved into the new house and me and my daughters pulled up I saw the same truck sitting on the corner. I sat there in the car for a second waiting to see if the truck was going to pull off and it didn't until I pulled off to go around the block. Once I got around the block the truck was nowhere in sight. I didn't stay at home that night cause I wasn't sure who was in that truck and I had the girls with me. So I drove to Chester to go to my dad's house."

"One day I was at Raheem house and the that same truck drove slow down the street before you drive into the gate of Raheem's house. Lisa, how do you know that it's the same truck? Asked Kyle, Kyle I have a screen shot picture of the license plate, each time I see the truck I make sure I look at the plate and it's the same plate each time. The one day when I was at your aunts house sitting outside I saw the truck and thought to myself that it was the detectives watching me, so I stop thinking about that it could be anyone else," explains Lisa.

"Wow this is crazy Lisa, and why are you just now telling me about this?" "Kyle I'm going to be honest with you, I didn't trust anyone, I didn't know who killed Jimmy and to me everyone was a suspect," laughed Lisa.

CHAPTER NINE

So the weekend is here and Lisa drops the girls off with Terri. Lisa please be careful, Kyle called and told me the conversation you and him had. Terri I will be extra careful. Lisa gets into her car and heads her way to give Ms Bianca a visit. The whole time she is driving she sees the black truck like 3 cars behind her, now Lisa is thinking should I leave this truck or should I let it follow me to where I am going just in case that it is the police.   Lisa pulls up to the gate, she rings the bell and Bianca buzzy her in, once Lisa get through the gate she looks out her rearview mirror again to see where the truck went to. She didn't see the truck anywhere in sight so she kept driving up the long drive way. Once she got out of the car she sees Bianca standing in the door waiting for her.

Before Lisa gets out of the car she puts her gun in her purse and gets out of the car, she walks slow to the front door. Bianca looked like she was crying for days, her eyes were all puffy and swallon. "Hey girl," says Lisa as she got close to Bianca, "hey Lisa, I'm glad that you were able to come and talk to me." "Sure," says Lisa as she gives her a look. They walk into the house and into the living room where both ladies sat down on the sofa.

"So what's up?" asked Lisa, Bianca cleared her throat before she began to talk. She begins telling Lisa that her Nook were 1st cousins, that their mother's were sisters. She tells Lisa how when she 1st saw Jimmy that she had fell in love with him, how she wanted to be his girl from the day she saw him but he paid her no mind. Lisa sits up, "Bianca I hear what you're saying but what does this have to do with you and Raheem?. What does it have to do with him taking all of his belongs and moving out?, she asked.

Bianca clear her throat again, "Lisa I am going to get to that in a second. I just 1st need to tell you what is going on and it will lead to what our broke up was about she said with tears in her eyes." "Okay go on," says Lisa.

"So I told my cousin Narlyn that I will bet her that I will get Jimmy before she would. But some how Jimmy found out about the bet, at 1st he didn't have any interest in Narly either. So the day of the party down at OD park when I saw my cousin all up in his face I decided to go after his boy Raheem. I knew when Jimmy gets drunk he like to take his girls to his mother house says Bianca, and Lisa I'm sure you know what happens from there," she said.

"So after the party, I was for sure that you were going to be the one that he was taking home with him because I seen him following you and his sister around the park, and how he was all up in your face. But when I seen him leaving with Narlyn before the party was over I knew she had won the bet." Lisa was tuned in to what Bianca was telling her. "Bianca did you know that Jimmy is older than me?, I was just 15 years old at that time and still was a virgin," says Lisa.

"Yes, I knew you was young Lisa but I really thought that you was at least 16 or 17. But anyway so I hooked up with Raheem that night to try and make Jimmy jealous. I knew that they were best friends and that they told each other everything from when me and my cousin would sit at the park with them and smoke weed."

"So Jimmy was hanging in Norristown asked Lisa?," "No, Jimmy would be up here when he wanted to be a whore," says Bianca. "Okay you never knew that Jimmy lived in Philly?," asked Lisa. "No" replied Bianca, "I knew that he hung in Philly a lot but didn't know that he lived down there." "Okay continue on with the story," says Lisa.

"When Raheem and I hooked up with each other a year later Raheem moved me out here with him cause I was pregnant," Bianca started crying, "Lisa I forced Jimmy to sleep with me, I got him drunk, I gave Raheem a sleeping pill and that's the night that Jimmy and I slept with each other. It was only one time, Jimmy really didn't want to do it but I forced him too." "Okay Bianca and how did you force him to have sex with you?," asked Lisa.

Bianca just looked at her, "Lisa I'm not really going to go into detail please just use you imagination. So 2 months later I ended up pregnant, I thought the baby was Jimmy's baby. I never told him or Raheem about this because I knew Jimmy would deny it. So that day you came her with the girls and you picked your daughter up, and Lisa once I saw that she looked just like Jimmy it gave me chills all through my body. Lisa all that I did to you I am so sorry about all of it."

"Okay Bianca, what did you do to me, all what you are telling me is way before Jimmy and I started messing with each other." Bianca put her head down, she was crying so much she couldn't get the next part of her story out. "Lisa the fire at your house was because of me, I had one of my cousins go to your house and throw a fire boom in the window, I am so sorry Lisa," cried Bianca.

Lisa crunched her hand into a tight fist, she wanted to beat the breaks off of Bianca, tears came to Lisa's eyes, "so you hated me for what Bianca?," says Lisa. "You hated me so much you wanted me and my daughters in the streets, what did I ever do to you Bianca". "When Jimmy and I got together I didn't even know who you was for a long time. It took Jimmy a whole year before he brought me to meet you and that's when you lived at the other house."

"WHAT ELSE IS GOING ON?," asked Lisa, "and what part does your girlfriend Tina play in?." "Tina just slept with Jimmy one time," says Bianca.   "Tina fell in love with Jimmy also and she wanted that relationship with him too but I put an end to that cause if I couldn't have him no one was going to have him," says Bianca. "That day Jimmy brought you to meet me he was all over you like a dog in heat, Lisa I was so jealous of you that I had to do something about it."

Bianca bent down to pick her ear ring up off the floor that fell out of her ear. Lisa eyes got real big, she started thinking I saw that ear ring somewhere and she remembered that ear ring looked just like the same one she found on the ground up there by the pizza shop.

"Bianca I'll ask a this question and please don't lie to me, why did Raheem pack his things and move out?, I mean you'll got into plenty of fights and he would just leave for a couple of days, but this time Bianca he took all of his things and left you?, can you tell me why?, asked Lisa.

Bianca couldn't stop crying, she picked her head up and said staring into Lisa eyes, "because I killed Jimmy," she said crying. Lisa pulled her gun from her purse and smacked Bianca across her face with the gun, but before she could swing again someone grabbed her hand, when Lisa turned around to see who it was she screamed JIMMY!!!! You're alive, Lisa started crying hugging him, Raheem walked in the door with the police. Normally Raheem would have had Bianca killed but he figured he would let her suffer in jail for the rest of her life.

The cops had already picked Nook and the cousin up that was supposed to meet Jimmy at the Pizza Shop to buy the drugs. Instead it was Bianca that showed up in all black that fired the shots at Jimmy's car. But she didn't kill Jimmy, Jimmy paid the cops to fake his death so he can find out who tried to kill him.

Jimmy hugged Lisa so tight and whispered in her ear, "baby you did it, you solved my murder."

The End

www.ingramcontent.com/pod-product-compliance
Lightning Source LLC
Chambersburg PA
CBHW071356200726
48294CB00004B/1189